To the Moon and Back for You

words by
Emilia Bechrakis Serhant

art by
EG Keller

Random House 🏠 New York

Library of Congress Cataloging-in-Publication Data is available upon request.
ISBN 978-0-593-17388-6 (trade) — ISBN 978-0-593-17389-3 (lib. bdg.) —
ISBN 978-0-593-17390-9 (ebook)

Book design by Nicole de las Heras

MANUFACTURED IN CHINA
10 9 8 7 6 5 4 3 2 1
First Edition

To my daughter, Zena.
You are the only one who knows
what my heart feels like on the inside.
Thank you for choosing me to be your mommy.
—E.B.S.

For Lori and Claire
—E.G.K.

I loved you before I met you.
I felt you in my arms before I could hold you.

But the road was long,

and the way was hard.

I went to the moon and back for you.

I navigated the roughest seas.

I climbed the tallest mountain.

When the desert was hottest, I crossed it.

When the tundra was coldest, I braved it.

When the winds were strongest,
I pushed through them.

It hurt, but that didn't stop me.

Every time I failed, I kept trying.
Every time I needed help, I reached for it.

I wanted you so badly.

Sometimes I thought
I'd never reach you.

But I never did give up.

Finding you was a journey . . .

. . . and meeting you was my greatest joy.

And now, my love,
we have each other.

The road was long, and the way was hard,
but I'd travel it again.

I would do it all over again.
For you.

AUTHOR'S NOTE

Ever since I was a little girl, I dreamed of being a mother. After my husband and I got married, we decided to try for a baby. I never imagined that becoming a mom would be so hard. Everyone around us seemed to be having a baby with such ease, but our road to parenthood was long and complicated. With each month and year that passed, I grew more heartbroken. And worse, I felt isolated. Was I the only one who felt afraid? Were other people struggling and hurting in the same way?

Determined to become a mother, I embarked on one of the most challenging, painful, and profound journeys of my life. It was a humbling cycle of losing hope and regaining it over and over again. After several years and multiple rounds of fertility treatments, including IVF, we finally conceived our precious baby. Through it all, I found faith and immense gratitude for those who helped me along the way. And the moment I laid eyes on my daughter, Zena, I knew this was the way I was meant to meet her. I knew I would go through it all over again just to have her.

There are so many ways to become a parent, and so many parents who struggle to get their baby. I wanted to write this book for those mothers and fathers who have had a similar road to parenthood. I wanted any parent to be able to share this story—my story, our story, your story—with their own miracle baby, to express how much they were wanted and loved before they even arrived.